D1233529

To: The amazing ladies of
WGRL. you Rock !

Saving Benjamin

Written By: Robbyne Kaamil

Illustrated by: Angel B. Motosky

XOXO XXX,

Dedicated to all the marine animals
who have been harmed or killed by ocean pollution

During a hot summer day
best friends Tiffany and Tyesha
were playing in their favorite spot
at the beach. It was also the place where
their friend Benjamin lived.

Benjamin was a beautiful fish with
bright colors and a big smile.
There was only one problem.
Benjamin couldn't play with his friends
Tiffany and Tyesha.

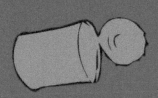

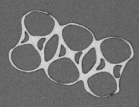

Benjamin lived in the ocean.
His mom wouldn't let him play in the ocean
because there was so much dangerous garbage
and plastic in the water.
These things could make Benjamin sick.

Sea animals often swallow plastic
and garbage because they mistake it
for food. Some of them get trapped
by things like soda can rings.

Benjamin couldn't swim near
the sea shore where Tiffany and Tyesha
liked to play.

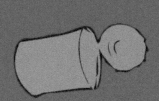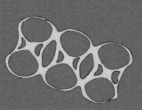

"Come on Benjamin.
Come play with us!" Tiffany yelled to him.
She and Tyesha were still
playing with their favorite beach ball.

Benjamin wanted to play.
"I can't play until there is
no more garbage in the water."

Benjamin saw a candy wrapper float past him.
"Oh, no!" Benjamin shouted and
went to hide under a rock.

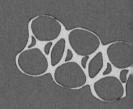

"What is wrong? It is just a wrapper!"
Tyesha laughed and pulled it from the water.
"It's small to you. But it is big to me."
Benjamin said from under the rock.
"Oh. I guess we never thought
about that!" She said.

This got the girls thinking.
"If we clean up the beach and
get rid of all the garbage
and plastic in the water would you
be able to come play with us?" They asked.
"I guess so!" Benjamin said.
He got so excited. Maybe one day soon
he could play with his friends.
He loved to splash in the water and swim.

"Where should we start?" Tiffany asked.
They looked at the beach
and saw all of the garbage.
"Oh no! This will be harder than
we thought," said Tyesha.

The girls started cleaning.
They used garbage bags
and picked up soda cans. lollipop sticks.
empty potato chip bags and plastic bottles.
They cleaned all day until the sun
started going down.

"Wow!" Tiffany said. "I think tomorrow Ben
will get to play with us!" They threw
all of the garbage they found into a
trash can and went home.
Tomorrow would be a great day.

They got up and went to the beach
the next afternoon.
"WHAT?!" They shouted in surprise.
The waves had brought even more
garbage than yesterday!
"Benjamin will never get
to play with us." said Tyesha.

"We just need more help!" Tiffany said.
She grabbed Tyesha's hand
and away they went to spread the word.

The girls talked to everyone they saw
on the beach. "Save the ocean. Don't litter!"
Tyesha shouted. "Don't throw plastic
in the ocean. It can hurt the fish!" Tiffany said.
Everyone passing by saw the girls and began
picking up garbage and putting it
where it belonged.

"It's working!" Tyesha said.
The girls were doing a good job
of making sure everyone knew
about the dangers of plastic and
garbage in the ocean.
They stayed at the beach all day.

"Hey!" Tiffany and Tyesha
heard a small voice call out to them.
"BENJAMIN!" They shouted
"My mom said tomorrow I can
come play with you!" Benjamin
was so excited he almost flew out of the
water and onto the sand.

The girls were so happy knowing
that they helped make the ocean
clean and safe for Benjamin.

The next day Tiffany and Tyesha
played with Benjamin near the seashore.
"Thank you for helping to
clean up the ocean for me."
Benjamin said as he
flipped into the air and wiggled his tail.

Every day Tiffany and Tyesha
went to visit Benjamin to make sure the
beach and ocean stayed clean and safe.
They always reminded people to be
friendly to the animals
who live in the sea and to take care of the ocean

This made Benjamin's mom
and all of his friends who lived
in the ocean very happy.

The end

CPSIA information can be obtained
at www.ICGtesting.com
Printed in the USA
BVOW05*0831040417
480014BV00009B/48/P